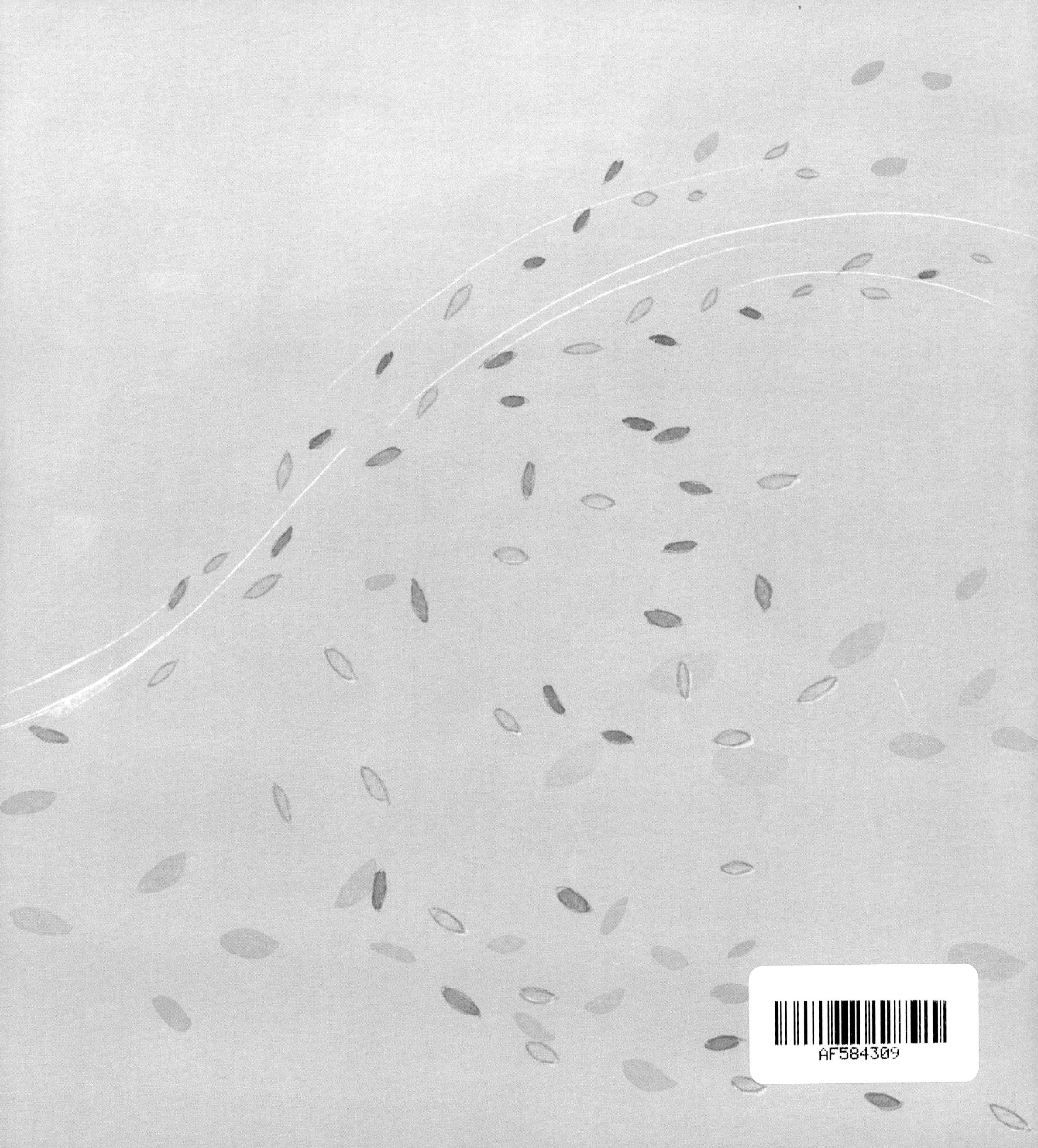
AF584309

For my darlings.
Keep on seeking. Grace hides all around - NG

With thanks to Nik, Arielle and Elsa - JR

Scholastic Press
An imprint of Scholastic Australia Pty Limited
PO Box 579 Gosford NSW 2250
ABN 11 000 614 577
www.scholastic.com.au

Part of the Scholastic Group
Sydney · Auckland · New York · Toronto · London · Mexico City
New Delhi · Hong Kong · Buenos Aires · Puerto Rico

Published by Scholastic Australia in 2024.

A catalogue record for this book is available from the National Library of Australia

ISBN: 978-1-76129-733-5 (hardback)

Jedda Robaard created these illustrations digitally.
Typeset in AgedBook.

Printed in China by RR Donnelley.
Scholastic Australia's policy, in association with RR Donnelley, is to use papers that are renewable and made efficiently from wood grown in responsibly managed sources, so as to minimise its environmental footprint.

10 9 8 7 6 5 4 3 2 1 24 25 26 27 28 / 2

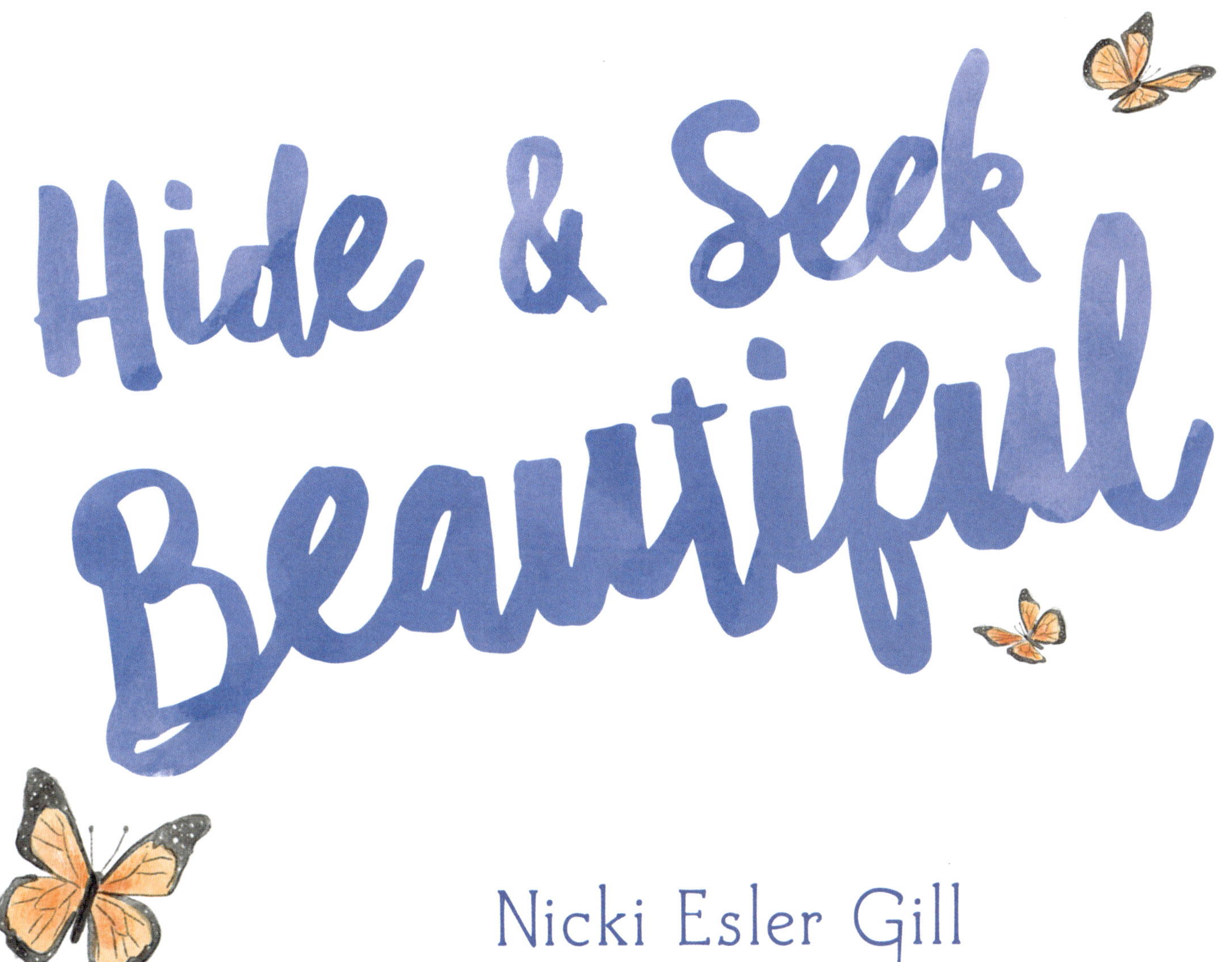

Nicki Esler Gill

Illustrated by
Jedda Robaard

A Scholastic Press book from Scholastic Australia

Annie and Boo had been friends since they were born.
Extra-special friends.

Of all the things they shared, Annie thought
that the most special was this:
they found the same things beautiful.

There was feet-in-mud beautiful. The squelch and suck and silky-cool between their toes.

There was big belly-laugh beautiful. Falling to the floor, clutching at stomachs. Hooting and hiccupping, happy tears streaming.

There was old Millie-Dog beautiful.
Warm, wet doggie breath that grown-ups said was 'Yuck!'

Heads together on her coat, feeling gentle breathing.

And there was being-together beautiful,
which Annie thought was best of all.

Being-together beautiful was
a friend to kiss her ouchies,
and make them fly away.

And it was being able to make
Boo all better, too.

It was knowing they were friends, even on days with cross words and turned backs, foot-stamping and huffy-storming.

It was raids on biscuit tins.

Dance parties. Tickle parties. Reaching too-high branches.

Yes, being together was the best kind of beautiful.

But then came goodbye.
And suddenly, all the beautiful felt harder to find.

One morning, missing Boo, Annie worked in the sandpit.
But even this was not much fun.

She smacked her castles down and flopped onto the sand.
She looked up at the sky.

At first, the sky seemed only grey, as grey as Annie felt.
But the longer she looked, the more she saw – the swirls of purple and whorls of white, and clouds trailing lazy above her.

Even on a grey old day, she saw
the sky was its own kind of beautiful.

It made her wonder whether beautiful was all around.
Maybe it was hiding, like Boo when they played hide-and-seek.
Maybe all you had to do was open your eyes
and search, and you would find it.

So Annie went searching for beautiful.

She found frost on the grass, an icing-sugar sprinkle.
Her footprints left behind were green on crunchy white.

And Mummy's cheeks kissed pink by cold.
And trees filled with wind, all the leaves dancing.

And drying dishes while Daddy washed,
with bubbles making a sink full of rainbows.

And heater-sitting, knees beneath her chin.
Being a girl-balloon, warm and filled with air.

Annie saw that she was right. She still missed Boo, with all her might. But hide-and-seek beautiful was everywhere, even in everyday things she hadn't thought special at all.

It filled up her heart to know that this was true.
It filled her heart with each new thing she found.

The day came at last.
And there she was, the same old Boo.

Later, after a dance party and a tickle party and a biscuit-tin raid, the girls went outside.

They lay down on their backs in the grass
and looked up at the sky.

And Annie showed Boo hide-and-seek beautiful.